Introduction

One uses the secret incantations of the Ancients, the mystical spells of the sorcerers, the magic handed down by the wise ones from the beginning of time.

The other uses the deadly tools of the knight, the weapons of attack and defense, the sword and the shield, the bludgeon and the dagger, forged in precious metal, created for his hands alone, to save lives—and to take lives.

Together, this man of magic and this man of the sword are known as the Wizard and the Warrior. Together, they have used their wisdom, their courage, and their awesome skills to defend Castle Silvergate and the kingdom of King Henry—to triumph over foes from this world and beyond.

By minstrel and by scribe, the tales are told of the foes they have faced: of the dragon Jebbarra from the twilight world between good and evil; of the Ghost Knights of Camelot and the Sorceress Morwenna; of the creatures from the Twisted Forest and the dragonbats from the Caves of Eternity.

But these foes are already vanquished, these

triumphs, a part of the past. Today brings new adventure to the Wizard and the Warrior—and new adventure to you. For you are about to enter their world; you are about to play a part in it.

Now you will be called upon to use *your* courage, *your* skill, and *your* wisdom. If you make the right decisions, the Wizard and the Warrior will triumph over all foes and their legend will shine on through history.

If you make the wrong choices, evil will triumph and their bright legend will dim. You will find yourself trapped in a world of ancient, unimagined horrors!

Are you ready to venture forth? The journey into the world of *Wizards, Warriors, and You* begins on PAGE 1.

WIZARDS, WARRIORS & YOU
is a game of fantasy role-playing.

In each adventure, you will choose to play the game as either the Wizard or the Warrior. Wearing the Wizard's robes, you will summon up magical spells to fend off your enemies. Carrying the Warrior's sword, you will use your strength and brilliance in battle to prevail against all challengers.

There are dozens of adventures in this book. If you choose to play the role of the Wizard, all of the mysterious spells in *The Book of Spells* at the back of this book will be at your command. Use them to guide the Wizard past peril after peril.

Then close the book and start all over again, this time as the Warrior. Try your skill with all of the weapons listed in *The Book of Weapons*, also found at the back of this book.

No matter which role you choose to play, you will face new challenges, battle surprising foes, and make life-or-death decisions!

Avon Books in the
WIZARDS, WARRIORS & YOU™ SERIES

WIZARDS, WARRIORS & YOU™

BOOK 12

The Scarlet Shield of Shalimar

by Scott Siegel & Barbara Siegel
illustrated by Earl Norem
A Parachute Press Book

AVON
PUBLISHERS OF BARD, CAMELOT, DISCUS AND FLARE BOOKS

To Nina and Ona Lacy
For bringing us together—
We dedicate this book of fantastic happenings
and magic to you because you brought something
fantastic and magical into our lives . . .
eternal love.

WIZARDS, WARRIORS & YOU™:
THE SCARLET SHIELD OF SHALIMAR
is an original publication of Avon Books. This
work has never before appeared in book form.

AVON BOOKS
A division of
The Hearst Corporation
1790 Broadway
New York, New York 10019

Copyright © 1986 by Parachute Press, Inc.
Published by arrangement with Parachute Press, Inc.
Library of Congress Catalog Card Number: 85-91194
ISBN: 0-380-89949-3

WIZARDS, WARRIORS & YOU™ is a trademark
of Parachute Press, Inc.

First Avon Printing, April 1986

AVON TRADEMARK REG. U. S. PAT. OFF. AND IN OTHER
COUNTRIES, MARCA REGISTRADA, HECHO EN U. S. A.

Printed in the U. S. A.

K-R   10 9 8 7 6 5 4 3 2 1

During the first cold days of autumn a fierce army of barbarians swept down out of the north. Wherever they roamed, they left a trail of fire and blood. And then—without any warning—they descended like locusts on King Henry's peaceful kingdom.

The leader of this savage horde, the seven-foot-tall Beladar, meant to crush King Henry's kingdom and rule it with an iron hand. As his huge army marched through the outlying farms and forests, the simple people of the countryside fled in terror, racing toward the protection of King Henry's Castle Silvergate. Here, there was refuge and hope for everyone. At least that's what they believed. . . .

Inside the castle, there was little food and even less water to feed the mass of frightened citizens. The barbarians had to be defeated. And quickly.

The King assembled his brave knights and gave them their orders: "The barbarians have assembled at the far end of the Plain of Cormack, outside the castle walls," he told them. "You must ride out with your swords held high and teach this Beladar a lesson he'll never forget. Show that undisciplined mob of savages the way warriors fight. Though Beladar's forces may outnumber you ten to one,"

King Henry added, "each knight of Castle Silvergate is worth *twenty* of the enemy."

After a flourish of trumpets the castle's drawbridge was let down, and a parade of knights rode proudly toward the field of battle, their plumes and banners flying in the air.

From the walls of the castle, the King watched with pride as his soldiers charged across the Plain of Cormack toward the enemy forces. "If only the Wizard and Warrior were here to take part in this great victory," Henry said to himself. "They will regret having missed this chance to partake in the glory that will be won this day."

As King Henry watched his knights ride out, he saw the huge barbarian, Beladar, hold up a jewel-encrusted shield. With a deafening bellow, Beladar rallied his savage horde against the defenders of Silvergate. But just before the two forces clashed at the center of the Plain of Cormack, the strange shield in Beladar's hand shot out a blinding scarlet light that cut like a red fire through the ranks of King Henry's grand army. And though no sword, no arrow, no lance had touched them, the knights fell from their mounts as if they had actually been vanquished in mortal combat!

Horrified, Henry saw the horses rear up in fear and bolt as the bright scarlet light swept across the field yet again. Before the battle had even begun, his knights were in full retreat. An ominous chant could be heard, growing ever louder, as the barbarians slowly marched toward the castle. "Beladar, the Conqueror!" they shouted. "Beladar, the Conqueror!"

The gates opened and what was left of King Henry's forces raced behind the safety of the castle walls. As the gates closed, locking the barbarians outside, Henry was forced to face the truth. Now there were only two people who could save his kingdom: the Wizard and the Warrior.

That night, under the cloak of darkness, the two friends returned to the castle from their battle with the Mountain Creatures of Wiskette. Knowing only that an army of barbarians surrounded Silvergate, they entered the castle through a secret underground passage and immediately sought an audience with their King.

"Your Grace," began the Warrior boldly, "why do you delay in attacking the army that lays siege to the kingdom?"

"I did not delay," the King replied angrily. "I attacked immediately and saw our brave knights destroyed by a strange scarlet light from their leader's shield."

The Wizard looked troubled. Softly, he asked, "Is their leader a giant of a man named Beladar?"

"Yes!" cried King Henry. "And his infernal army chanted 'Beladar, the Conqueror' as they surrounded the castle. You know this barbarian?"

"No," the Wizard admitted. "But I have heard of him. It was rumored that he somehow stole the Scarlet Shield of Shalimar from the holy spot in which it was buried."

"The Scarlet Shield of Shalimar?" questioned the Warrior.

"It is an enchanted shield, filled with great magic," explained the Wizard. "It was cast by Merlin's own hand, and its power is almost limitless!"

"It may possess powerful magic," the Warrior answered the Wizard, "but it can be no match for the combined strength of your great sorcery and my sword and dagger. Together," he boldy proclaimed, "we shall defeat this Beladar and return the shield to the sacred spot from which it was stolen."

"Aye," said the King, smiling for the first time since the defeat of his knights. "From your lips have come the very words I was about to command of you."

King Henry strode to the tall, narrow window of the throne room. "Out there," he said, "you see the campfires of Beladar's army. Before the morning light, you must make your way into his camp and somehow steal the sacred shield. Without its magic protection, Beladar's men cannot stand against our knights."

Both the Wizard and the Warrior knelt before Henry. "Good King," they vowed, "we will not fail you." But in their hearts they knew that if they faltered in their quest, Beladar would drown the kingdom in a sea of blood, and all that was good and noble would disappear beneath a red wave of death.

Thus the adventure begins. And now the story becomes *your* story, the mission to defeat Beladar becomes *your* mission. The time has come for you to choose the role you wish to play.

Will you take the part of the *Wizard* or the *Warrior?* Make your choice now.

If you choose to be the Wizard, turn to PAGE 9.
If you choose to be the Warrior, turn to PAGE 15.

Six close-set orange eyes, blazing like the flames of hell itself, stare right through you. Hundreds of long, thin arms with hands that claw the air dance in front of a large body covered with foot-long protective spikes.

In some ancient time, someone—perhaps Merlin himself—created this monster to protect the burial site of the Scarlet Shield and Sword. The demon seems to have no weakness. You marvel over the fact that the Warrior somehow survived his battle with this monster. But how will you fare?

The six orange eyes glow with an other-worldly light. You force yourself closer, hoping to learn if this demon is a living, breathing creature or if it's actually the creation of a magic spell. But before you can determine what powers it possesses, the thing in front of you suddenly sweeps twenty large rocks off the cave's floor and hurls them at you!

The stones come flying like an avalanche. Which spell will counter the creature's attack? If this being is made of flesh and blood, your Shrink spell might work. But if it's sorcery that you're up against, then your only hope is to fight it with Combat Magic. But be forewarned: If Combat Magic is your choice, this will be the *only* time you can use that spell.

If you want to defend yourself with the Shrink spell, turn to PAGE 78.

If you want to defend yourself with Combat Magic, turn to PAGE 24.

As you pull yourself up onto dry land, Beladar spots you. So much for the element of surprise!

The barbarian leader swings his Scarlet Shield around and points it right at you. You've got one second to either take the offensive or find a way to avoid the magic of the shield.

The only weapon that could conceivably save you is your Flying Spear (Weapon #9). If it's one of the weapons you chose to take with you, throw it straight and true—and then immediately turn to PAGE 57 to see if you hit your mark.

If you don't have the Flying Spear, dive back into the moat, and find out if you dove in fast enough—and deep enough—on PAGE 63.

8

You step back into the ruins and stand guard with the Warrior, doing your best to keep the barbarians from streaming into the castle. And there, in a cloud of dust from the crumbling walls, you see the glow of the Scarlet Shield.

Beladar is coming to you!

"Mighty Sword," you speak aloud, "this is the moment when your magic must be supreme."

You advance toward Beladar, oblivious to the battle around you. And that is your greatest mistake. Three barbarians have gotten behind you. The Warrior sees them and shouts a warning. Too late. A lance pierces your back while a dagger strikes you in the back of the neck. You fall to the ground just as Beladar steps out of the cloud of dust. From your limp hand he plucks the Scarlet Sword of Shalimar.

Instead of slaying him, you have given Beladar the power to conquer humanity. With both the shield and the sword, he'll turn the world scarlet with blood—until you choose once more to open this book and give this tragic tale a new . . .

END

Instructions for the Wizard:

The Scarlet Shield of Shalimar was created by the most powerful wizard the earth has known. It is an object of rare and deadly magic—a force that will challenge your own magic beyond anything you have ever encountered. You will need all of your skills and spells, Wizard, to recover the Scarlet Shield from the barbarian, Beladar.

At the back of this book, on page 97, you will find a book of all the magical spells you've learned through the years. Turn now to *The Book of Spells*. Read it over carefully to remind yourself of the special powers you possess.

Now turn to **PAGE 11** to begin your quest for the Scarlet Shield.

Beladar squeezes your throat until you can no longer breathe. There are only seconds before you will black out. You force yourself to stay conscious, focusing on the shield in his other hand—and the sight of it gives you a desperate idea.

In your last moment of consciousness you decide to cast the spell of Shift Shape. But you may not have enough strength to make your spell effective. Will chance be with you?

Flip a coin twice. If you get heads both times or tails both times, turn to PAGE 22.

If you get heads once and tails once, turn to PAGE 36.

In the stillest hours of the night, you and the Warrior hurry back toward the secret passage that will take you out beyond the castle walls.

"The Scarlet Shield will be closely guarded," says the Warrior.

"Yes," you reply thoughtfully. "Beladar will not let it out of his sight. But a wizard can play tricks on what the eye can see."

The Warrior smiles. "You have a plan?"

Entering the long, dark tunnel that ends at the edge of the river, you turn back to the Warrior and say, "With luck, we'll have the Scarlet Shield of Shalimar in our hands within the hour."

In the inky blackness of the tunnel there is the sudden clash of rattling steel, the unmistakable sound of swords being drawn from scabbards—and the harsh voice of a barbarian right in front of you booms with laughter.

"With luck, you say? Well, your luck has just run out!"

You can hear the whistling sound of the barbarian's blade cutting through the air. In less than a second you'll have a very split personality—as well as a split body. Only one of your spells can keep you alive and in one piece. And you must make your choice immediately!

If you choose Spell #2, Forest Imp's Freeze, turn to PAGE 14.

If you choose Spell #3, Conjurer's Confusion, turn to PAGE 18.

12

When you reach down for the Whistling Mace, you're shocked to find instead a simple musical instrument!

You have no weapon, but you quickly ask yourself if perhaps there is a reason why it was replaced by this odd wooden object. With nothing to lose, you lift the musical instrument to your lips and blow.

What comes out is a strange high-pitched whistle—identical to the sound made by the Whistling Mace—and when the dragon hears that tone, it instantly falls asleep! Quickly, you race past the sleeping colossus and grab the Scarlet Sword of Shalimar.

And then you wake up! The island is the way you first found it: completely empty, flat, and covered with a low-hanging mist. But one thing is very much changed: *The Scarlet Sword of Shalimar is now yours!*

Unfortunately, there is no time to celebrate your victory. Now you must find your way back to King Henry's kingdom.

Turn to PAGE 47.

Merlin told the Wizard that the Scarlet Sword was buried at the highest point on the island. With that thought in mind, you slowly drift down into the mist and look around.

The Island of Dreams is a land of strange noises and even stranger sights. What makes it so strange is that the island seems to be completely empty. There are no trees, no rocks, no animals, no rivers, no streams—nothing! Just a layer of sand draped in fog—and an unmistakable sense of enchantment everywhere. Yet you can faintly hear the roar of a waterfall, the wind blowing through trees, the murmur of animals deep in the forest, and the buzz of insects in the air. It seems incredible, but it isn't just the dragon who guards the Scarlet Sword that can't be seen—*everything on the Island of Dreams is invisible!*

Or is it?

This island has its name for a reason. Maybe you can't see anything because you're awake. Perhaps if you went to sleep you would see the real island in your dreams. But then there is another possibility: In this realm of magic maybe you are already asleep and what you see now is all a dream! Which is it?

If you think you should try to find the Scarlet Sword in your dreams, turn to PAGE 32.

If you think you're already dreaming and can now find the Scarlet Sword, turn to PAGE 46.

You chant the strange-sounding words of the spell, and then wait for the barbarian's blade to freeze in midair. But it doesn't! The sword is still coming at you. At the very last instant you realize your mistake—the Forest Imp's Freeze works only when the object of the spell is clearly in view. In the tunnel's total darkness, you can't see the enemy swordsman even though he stands directly in front of you.

The blade comes crashing down. If you were still alive, you'd have not one, but two headaches . . . because you now have two heads. Unfortunately, each of those heads is only half the size of the original.

As you can see, two heads aren't always better than one in the land of *Wizards, Warriors, and You.*

END

Instructions for the Warrior:

You have fought countless invading forces, but none of them has ever possessed a weapon like the Scarlet Shield of Shalimar. To take the Scarlet Shield from Beladar will require strategy and cunning as well as all of your formidable battle skills.

At the back of this book, on page 101, you will find a book of all the weapons you possess. Turn now to *The Book of Weapons*. In addition to the Sword of the Golden Lion, which is always with you, you may take *only three* of these weapons along with you on your mission. Choose carefully. Decide which weapons you will take.

Now turn to PAGE 17 and begin the quest for the Scarlet Shield of Shalimar.

FOREVER

WARRIOR

The Wizard's words make you stop and think. And in those few moments spent pondering your friend's advice, two barbarian scouts stumble upon your hiding place!

Before you can draw your sword from its scabbard, one of the scouts stabs the Wizard in the back with a dagger. Enraged, you jump to your feet and, bare-handed, kill the soldier who's slain your friend.

The second scout attacks you with a spear, striking your right shoulder. He grins as he sees that he's wounded you, but when you back away he loses his weapon because it's still stuck in your body. That gives you a chance to draw your sword, but it isn't on the scout that you'll need to use it. Out of the corner of your eye you see Beladar stalking you with a cutlass in one hand and the Scarlet Shield of Shalimar in the other.

Turn to PAGE 75.

You and the Wizard are about to take the secret passageway out of the castle when suddenly, from the eastern watchtower, you hear a sentry cry, "The barbarians are attacking!"

The entire castle jumps to frantic life as King Henry's knights race up to the parapets to repel the invaders. But the warning has come far too late. Already the barbarians have thrown up crude wooden ladders and are climbing the castle walls. Caught off guard, Silvergate is in terrible danger of a quick and bloody capture.

"The campfires we saw from King Henry's window were a trick!" exclaims the Wizard.

"Yes," you angrily admit. "A trick that might very well mean our doom."

What should you do? Is your first duty to protect the castle? Or should you still try to find Beladar behind enemy lines and fight him for possession of the Scarlet Shield of Shalimar? The fate of the kingdom rests on the decision you must make. Let us hope that you choose wisely.

If you choose to stay and fight, turn to PAGE 44.

If you choose to follow your original plan and search for the Scarlet Shield, turn to PAGE 25.

You draw your cloak around you and utter two ancient words that bring the spell of Conjurer's Confusion into being. . . .

"What am I doing?" cries the barbarian, stopping his sword in midflight.

"Beware!" you call, taking advantage of his muddled mind. "The men behind you are your enemies!"

He wheels around and screams in defiance, "Then I will kill every one of them!" And then, without any hesitation, he charges headlong into his own troops.

In the darkness you hear wild yells and the clash of swords in fierce battle. The barbarians are almost as confused by their leader's actions as he is by your spell.

But the bloody battle in the tunnel is blocking your way. You've got to infiltrate Beladar's camp before the sun rises or you will have no chance of stealing the Scarlet Shield of Shalimar.

You are forced to take a desperate gamble. Casting the spell to Move Time Forward, you hope that neither you nor the Warrior will suddenly find yourself in a deadly time and place from which there will be no escape. . . .

Where in the future will the spell take you? To discover your fate, flip a coin five times.

If it comes up heads three or more times, turn to **PAGE 27**.

If it comes up tails three or more times, turn to **PAGE 39**.

When all trace ot Merlin's spirit has vanished, you go to tell King Henry and the Warrior what you have learned.

"Well," says the King after you have finished, "I have heard stranger things from you, Wizard."

"And I," says the Warrior, undaunted. "We must leave Silvergate at once and begin our quest for the Scarlet Sword."

"That is no easy matter," you reply. "The place known as Shalimar lies atop a treacherous mountain that is shrouded in mists and magic. The journey there is long, and once we actually reach the mountain we must pass beyond the enchantments to the hiding place of the sword."

"I'll have horses made ready—" the King begins.

"Sire," you say, trying to sound calmer than you feel, "I think we had best travel by the powers of magic."

Turn to PAGE 92.

20

With your arms outspread, you ram into all three barbarians before they can throw their spears. Knocked from their ladders, they go flying back, head over heels, and tumble down into the moat below.

Unfortunately, the barbarians aren't the only ones to go for an unexpected swim. The momentum of your charge carries you over the castle wall, and you, too, go sailing down into the moat's murky waters. And that's the least of your problems. Now you're on the outside of the castle, an easy target for thousands of bloodthirsty barbarian soldiers.

You've got to get back inside the castle walls.

But before you can swim a single stroke, something catches your eye. In a silver chariot led by four magnificent black horses, it is Beladar himself racing toward the castle gate. And he is holding the Scarlet Shield of Shalimar! Now that his first line of troops has breached the castle walls, he is leading the main charge that might very well overrun King Henry's forces.

As Beladar's chariot draws closer you realize that this may be your chance to take the Scarlet Shield— or find life itself taken from you. But you have always lived your life as a warrior, so despite the odds against you, you decide to take the risk. And—make no mistake—the odds are against you!

Flip a coin ten times. If tails come up seven or more times, turn to PAGE 7.

If tails come up less than seven times in ten flips, turn to PAGE 31.

You summon all of your remaining power, and just as Beladar begins to squeeze the last breath from your body, you cast the spell of Shift Shape—and suddenly Beladar finds himself holding *two* Scarlet Shields. Startled, he drops both and stares down at them in bewilderment. In the deep red haze of the tent he can't decide which is the real shield and which is the fake!

With a scream of frustrated rage, Beladar grabs two blazing torches. "It is well known that the Scarlet Shield will not burn," he cries, "but perhaps the impostor will!"

At Beladar's cry the Warrior slashes through the back of the tent with the Sword of the Golden Lion. "Are my eyes deceived?" you hear him mutter. "Here are not one but *two* Scarlet Shields."

"You are skilled at counting," Beladar snaps, swinging the torches at the Warrior. But with lightning reflexes, the Warrior ducks beneath the flaming weapons, grabs one of the shields, and dashes out of the tent.

In the middle of the camp, nearly one hundred barbarians move in for the attack. In the Warrior's right hand is his famous sword and in his left, the shield that he hopes will bring salvation to the kingdom. As they close in, the barbarians spot the shield. They know what it can do. They've seen the death and destruction it has caused in Beladar's hands. The field goes suddenly quiet as the barbarians drop their weapons and flee in blind terror.

Turn to PAGE 79.

You watch as the Warrior, his Bludgeon raised, chases the now-tiny creature. Sure that he will have no further trouble with this foe, you begin hurriedly to dig for the Scarlet Sword. When you're just six inches below the surface, the ground begins to take on a reddish hue. You're getting close!

You hear the sound of someone breathing behind you. "I think I have found it!" you call out to your old friend.

Suddenly, something falls on the ground next to you—the crumpled body of the Warrior! You wheel around and see the demon—*once again at full size*—and that, Wizard, is the last thing you ever see in this life. Your spell lasted only long enough to get the both of you killed!

You came so close to getting the Scarlet Sword. Now you and the Warrior lie buried next to the prize you never captured. At least you will rest undisturbed—under the six watchful eyes of the guardian of Shalimar.

END

In the time it takes to create a thought, you summon every bit of power that exists in your soul, invoking the most awesome magic that a living being can create. The muscles in your body quiver as if lightning instead of blood courses through your veins. And then you feel the enormous strength of the sorcery . . . and you unleash it!

The stones disappear. The creature vanishes. You're alone in the Demon's Lair—but the demon is no more.

Ah, but though you chose the right spell, your victory has left you totally exhausted. You barely manage to dig the Scarlet Sword out of the ground. When the dirt is cleared away, you see that its blade is bathed in a crimson glow, and the ruby-encrusted gold handle seems to sparkle like sunlight on the surface of a lake.

The Scarlet Sword is finally yours, but in your weakened condition, how are you going to get it back to the kingdom in time to save your homeland? You will not be able to use your magic for a full day.

You sit on the cold ground, holding the Scarlet Sword of Shalimar in your hands, and you think: Could the sword itself provide the magic you need in your stead? It seems to glow a deeper red as if to give you its answer. The truth is that you have no choice. The Scarlet Sword is your only hope.

To discover if the Scarlet Sword can help you, flip a coin once. If it turns up heads, turn to PAGE 43.
If it turns up tails, turn to PAGE 49.

"There is only one way to stop this attack," you tell the Wizard. "We must find Beladar and take possession of the Scarlet Shield."

Together you continue out through the secret passageway and emerge behind the lines of the charging enemy. Up on the crest of a hill the red gleam of the shield catches your eye. Beladar stands alone there, watching the progress of his army.

You can hardly believe your good fortune. With no lookouts to warn Beladar of your presence, it seems the perfect opportunity to attack. Still, you try to control your excitement as you tell the Wizard, "I will get as close to Beladar as I can by crawling through the high grass. Then, when the moment is right, I'll take him."

"I am not so sure that's a sound plan," says your friend worriedly. "Beladar seems supremely confident. There may be a very good reason why he has no guards around him. Perhaps we should stay here and watch him a little longer."

Beladar remains where he is, absorbed by the sight of his army. When a red fox darts by him and he takes no notice of it, you realize that he is completely unaware of what surrounds him. There is no doubt in your mind. Now is the moment—*unless* you choose to heed the Wizard's words of caution. If he's right, his advice could save your life. If he's wrong, you might lose your only chance to save the kingdom.

If you choose to heed the Wizard's warning, turn to PAGE 16.

If you want to take this chance and attack Beladar, turn to PAGE 33.

The next thing you see is King Henry's kingdom. But what you behold both saddens and angers you. The north and west corners of the castle are burning, there are massive cracks in the walls, and the big oak gate has been battered off its hinges. You wonder what has become of the Wizard. If you survive, will you find him alive or dead?

There is no time left for wondering. Beladar and his barbarian horde are about to make their final assault. And there you stand, alone, in the middle of the battlefield, facing a charging army led by a giant who holds within his hands the power of the Scarlet Shield of Shalimar.

But you have the Scarlet *Sword!*

You raise the magic weapon, gleaming in all its red glory, and command it to stop the onrushing enemy troops. The sword obeys by throwing out a wave of scarlet light that forms a ten-foot-high glowing red wall!

The barbarians charge right into it—but they never come out the other side. Thousands of soldiers disappear in the wall of red light, swallowed alive by a magic too great for any mere mortal to survive. With screams of terror, the rest of the barbarian army retreats. Only Beladar, with the Scarlet Shield in front of him, can walk through the deadly red wall. And when he does, it's just the two of you: sword against shield, good against evil, life against death.

You are a warrior and this is what you live for. But it might also be what you die for. Let the battle begin!

Grip the Scarlet Sword tightly and then turn to **PAGE 35.**

The darkness of the tunnel disappears. You are standing behind the largest tent in the enemy camp, no doubt the tent of Beladar . . . and perhaps the location of the magic shield.

The night is quickly fading into dawn, but that no longer matters. You feel certain that you are close to your goal.

"Stay here and keep watch," you whisper to the Warrior, "while I go inside and search for the shield."

The Warrior nods, drawing his Sword of the Golden Lion. You know that he will do his utmost to protect you from anyone or anything outside of Beladar's tent. But you, and you alone, will have to protect yourself from whatever waits inside.

Silently, you work your way to the tent's entrance and take a quick look around. You are pleased that the camp is quiet. Everyone is asleep except the guards whose eyes are locked on Castle Silvergate on the hill high above the river.

Gingerly now, you open the tent flaps and peer inside. There's a strange scarlet haze, like a red fog, glowing within. You step inside, closing the flaps firmly behind you. . . .

Turn to PAGE 34.

28

The Wizard raises an eyebrow, but tactfully makes no comment on your appearance. "I have been looking for you," he says. "And though I am grateful that you are safe, I fear I will be sending you into danger once again. What I am about to ask of you may be the impossible. Believe me, I would not have it this way. . . ."

"Speak your mind," you gently tell your old friend. "We have often done the impossible. Perhaps we can do it again."

The Wizard takes a deep breath and explains: "I summoned the ghost of Merlin to ask if there was any power that could defeat the Scarlet Shield of Shalimar. He spoke to me and said, 'Only the Scarlet Sword of Shalimar is the equal of the Scarlet Shield. It, too, was cast by my hand, and it holds within its blade the magic of the ages. It is buried at the highest point on the sacred Island of Dreams, and guarded there by an invisible dragon.'"

"Then we must go there at once and find this Scarlet Sword!" you declare.

Go on to PAGE 29.

"Not *we*," says the Wizard. "You. This time I cannot go with you. It is beyond my sorcery. I can send only one of us to the Island of Dreams with my Flight spell. It is pointless for me to go, as the island lies so far within the realm of magic that after casting this spell I would be left too weak to win the sword. But *you* could do it. And if you can defeat the invisible dragon, you must somehow find a way to use the enchantment of the island to return home quickly with the Scarlet Sword." With a sigh, he adds, "I am sorry that I can do no more than this to help you on your quest."

"Do not despair, my friend," you offer kindly. "And do not delay. Cast your spell now and send me to the Island of Dreams. And if fate is kind to me, I shall quickly return with the weapon that will save the kingdom!"

Turn to PAGE 38 . . . and soar on the wings of magic!

30

Standing on the castle ramparts, you cast the spell to Command Animals. All is quiet.

The Warrior glances up into the clouds and then back at you. "Nothing is happening," he complains.

"Be patient, my friend," you answer with a knowing grin. "Nature's magic is about to swoop down out of the sky."

At just that moment, two giant eagles dive gracefully out of the clouds and land nearby with a great flapping of wings.

"I should know better than to doubt you," the Warrior shamefacedly concedes as each of you climb on the back of one of the enormous eagles.

"You have saved my life far too many times to ever have to apologize to me," you reply. And then the two of you, upon your feathered steeds, take flight toward the destiny that awaits you.

Turn to PAGE 48.

You've made up your mind, and you begin swimming toward the edge of the moat near the castle gate. It is from here that you'll make your surprise attack on Beladar. Except that, as things turn out, you're the one who is surprised. Remember the three barbarians you knocked into the moat? Well, one of them comes up from behind you and grabs you around the throat!

He pulls you down into the water's dark depths.

And you never come up. Ever.

Close the book. Even a Warrior needs a breather—especially after an eternity without any air.

END

32

You lie down on your side and close your eyes. But you are so anxious to find the Scarlet Sword that it's hard to fall asleep. Still, you have to try. This may be the only way to save the kingdom—and time must surely be running out. How much longer can King Henry's forces keep Beladar at bay?

Finally, you begin slowly to drift into that netherworld that exists between waking and sleep. As you lie there you hear the hungry growl of a nearby animal. Is it one of the invisible creatures of the island? Or is it that the sounds you hear are heralding your approach to the dreamworld?

You hear the growl again. It seems louder . . . closer. If you could, you'd jump to your feet and fight whatever is stalking you, but it's too late. You have now crossed over into the world of dreams . . . or is it the world of nightmares?

Turn to PAGE 40.

You crawl through the tall grass, slowly edging nearer to the barbarian leader. Although Beladar is facing in your direction, he hasn't spotted you. Suddenly, one of his men calls out, and he turns and looks away. This is your chance! You jump to your feet and charge up the hill. But that's when the Scarlet Shield of Shalimar suddenly shoots bolts of lightning in every direction!

And that's why Beladar didn't need any guards!

A lightning bolt strikes your sword and you come to a sudden, shocking . . .

END

You can feel the power of the shield. Its magic seems to fill the tent the way a strong wind fills the sails of a ship. And rightly so, because you're about to set sail on a sorcerer's journey. . . .

As you reach for the shield the red haze within the tent grows thick and heavy, blinding you, making it almost impossible to breathe. You grope through the scarlet fog, trying to find the shield. The tent walls, the ground beneath your feet, and the shield itself all seem to vanish in the mist.

There! In the haze! You see something move, but you can't make out the shape. You step toward the shimmering light, and out of the brightness a hand reaches out and closes around your throat.

"I am Beladar!" says a hard, cold voice. "The shield does my bidding. It protects me and I protect it. It lives in the white light of my greatness and I live in the red light of its magic. And you," he continues softly, "are about to face the black light of death."

Quickly, if you're wearing something with red in it, turn to **PAGE 10**.

If you're not wearing anything red, turn to **PAGE 89**.

As he lumbers in close to you, Beladar snarls, "You shall die like all the others who have stood in my way. My power will overwhelm you!"

"The power is not yours," you reply. "It belongs only to the shield."

"It matters not," he growls, "as long as the shield is in my hands. And as for you, you shall soon be in your grave!"

And with that, he orders his shield to cut off the arm that holds your sword. A thin shaft of red light shoots across the short distance between you. Quickly, you raise the magic blade and hold it right out in front of your body . . . and the shaft of light is sliced in half so that it flows around you on either side.

Beladar is clearly astonished.

You allow yourself the small pleasure of a smile and say, "Perhaps I will not die as easily as you imagined."

"Oh, you shall die," Beladar confidently replies. "And you shall die now!"

Under cover of a blinding flash of red light, the barbarian creates five identical images of himself. You face six enemies who look exactly alike. Whom will you fight?

If you trust the Scarlet Sword to tell you which of the six images of Beladar is the real one, turn to PAGE 74.

If you'd rather create five duplicate images of yourself to fight Beladar's illusions, turn to PAGE 82.

36

You are too weak, Wizard. The mental powers needed to cast the Shift Shape spell are far beyond your waning strength. The spell you ultimately conjure up is one of the first things you ever learned as a wizard—and Beladar laughs as birds begin flying out of your cape.

Under other circumstances you also might laugh. But the dead are not known for a sense of humor. You've gone to a sorcerer's heaven, a place where only the magic of opening a special book can bring you back to life. And that book is *Wizards, Warriors, and You*.

END

Drawing your cloak around you, you begin to cast your spell. At first the air is still, but then the wind suddenly whips up behind you, carrying you and the Warrior to the west—directly toward Shalimar!

The two of you soar on the cutting edge of the fierce wind, like foam at the crest of a wave just before it crashes on the shore. But you aren't crashing. You're taken ever higher, ever farther, sweeping across the sky on great gusts of air.

It is not long before the Warrior points ahead and cries, ''The Mountain of Shalimar!''

''I see it!'' you shout back, pleased with the enormous distance you have traveled so quickly.

You get closer and closer. Now you near the top of the mountain. . . .

Turn to PAGE 65.

38

The Wizard casts the spell of Flight, and you fly upward, into the clouds and across the horizon. The land below races by, and soon you realize you are no longer above the earth as we know it, but flying through the realm of magic. Below you lies a great body of silver water. And there, on the surface of the water, sits a small circle of heavy mist.

Legend has it that the Island of Dreams cannot be seen from afar because it is always covered with a fog. Still, you have no way of knowing for sure if the island you seek is actually there . . . until a monstrous vulture with two heads and twelve deadly talons angrily flies up out of the fog to fight for its territory. Now you're sure that the Island of Dreams is below because your hideous-looking enemy is something out of a nightmare!

There is no doubt in your mind that this fiendish monster could tear you to pieces before you ever set foot on the Island of Dreams. With a horrible shrieking sound, it attacks. Defend yourself—if you can!

If you have brought the Bludgeon, and want to use it, turn to PAGE 67.

If you are armed with the Cutlass of Cornwell or if you wish to use your sword, turn to PAGE 54.

Flash! The magic that moves time forward surrounds you.

The sun has just risen and both you and the Warrior are standing in plain sight, right in the middle of the enemy encampment!

A cry of "Intruders!" blasts the early-morning calm. Instantly, the camp comes alive and before you know it at least one thousand of the barbarian troops have encircled you—with their lances and daggers raised high, they're coming in for the kill!

The Warrior bravely draws his sword, but even he can't defeat a thousand soldiers. No, your magic got you into this mess, and now you must somehow use your magic to find a way out.

But you will not leave without the Scarlet Shield of Shalimar. Your duty to your King means far more to you than your life. You know that to use sorcery solely for the purpose of saving your skin would bring the blackest dishonor upon your soul.

Boldly, then, you call out, "Why does Beladar hide? If he does not fear us, let him come forward!"

The advancing troops stop dead in their tracks. No one has ever questioned the courage of their leader. And each man is now asking himself, "Who are these two beings who ignore the certain death of a thousand spears and arrows, and who instead demand to see the dreaded Beladar?"

They're about to find out. Turn to PAGE 42.

40

In your dream, the island is a lush jungle and you are standing near a waterfall at the bottom of the island's tallest mountain. Then you hear that loud, hungry growl again. . . .

You whirl around, drawing your sword from its scabbard, expecting to see a huge, wild animal ready to spring. Instead, you see a furry little creature about the size of a newborn kitten—with the loudest growl you have ever heard!

Out of the small pouch of food that you always carry you take a chunk of cheese and give it to the odd little animal. It takes the cheese in its tiny mouth and quickly scampers away into the underbrush.

You look back up at the mountain. That is where the Scarlet Sword of Shalimar must be. And that is where you must go. Because this is a dream, you are able to climb to the top in the blink of an eye. But when that blink is over, you come face to face with the guardian of the Scarlet Sword: a hundred-foot-tall dragon that breathes not fire but ice!

The Scarlet Sword is lying on a rock in plain view behind the dragon. But also in plain view are those who came before you—knights, kings, maidens, sorcerers— all frozen forever in blocks of ice. You have no doubt that all of them tried—and failed— to capture the Scarlet Sword. Will your destiny be as bleak and cold?

Turn to PAGE 55.

42

The seven-foot-tall leader of the barbarians emerges from the largest tent in the camp. He has an angry scowl on his face, but you take no notice of that. All you see is that in his right hand he carries the bejeweled Scarlet Shield of Shalimar!

"Beladar hides from no one," the giant says in an ominously low voice. "The two of you will die slow, cruel deaths for your insult to my name."

Unshaken by his threat, you reply, "Your name deserves far greater insults than I can devise. You have destroyed homes, enslaved the peaceful, and killed the innocent—and you did all of this with a shield you stole from its sacred place of burial."

"Enough!" booms the voice of Beladar, enraged by your impudence. "The shield is mine! It belongs to he who is strong enough to hold it and to no one else. And I am the strongest!" Beladar's voice softens, becoming even more deadly. "I promise you, Wizard, with this shield I will conquer not just this wretched kingdom, but the entire kingdom of man on earth!"

"We shall see about that," you reply as you prepare to cast a spell. Which shall it be—magic of the earth or the air?

If you choose Spell #5, Sorcerer's Sleep, turn to PAGE 60.

If you choose Spell #9, Flight, turn to PAGE 72.

"Let your magic serve us," you say softly to the glowing Scarlet Sword, "and bring us to the land of King Henry so that we may do battle against Beladar."

The sword responds with a sudden flash of blinding red light!

When you can see again, what will your eyes behold? Blink three times and then hurry to **PAGE 73**!

What good is the shield if the kingdom is destroyed? In your mind there can be no other choice. You must remain here and drive the barbarians from the castle walls. Then, and only then, will you continue your mission in search of the Scarlet Shield.

With the Sword of the Golden Lion in your hand, you charge to the ramparts, ready for battle. A barbarian carrying a long dagger in each hand rushes you from behind. Only at the last moment do you sense his presence and turn. He's right on top of you, his first dagger inches from your chest—but you cleverly dodge the blow, and his blade clangs harmlessly against your steel helmet. Before he can swing the second dagger, you run him through with your sword.

Your attacker slumps over, but as you pull your sword from his dead body, three more barbarians climb to the top of the wall, each of them holding a spear aimed at your heart. Quickly—how will you defend yourself?

If you brought the Triple Crossbow (Weapon #4) with you, go on to PAGE 45.

If you didn't bring the Triple Crossbow, take a chance and leap right at them before they can throw their spears—and find out how well you fared on PAGE 20.

The Triple Crossbow is in your hands within an instant, loaded and ready. You fire all three arrows toward the barbarians climbing over the wall.

You hear three thuds as your arrows hit their marks, sending the invaders falling back over the wall. But the three barbarians are immediately replaced by the glow of a red light that grows brighter and brighter as it approaches. You're sure it must be Beladar carrying the Scarlet Shield of Shalimar as he scales the castle wall.

This could be your chance to pluck the shield out of Beladar's hands before he can conquer the kingdom. All you have to do is reach down over the castle wall and grab it—that is, *if it is the Scarlet Shield*.

You must take the chance . . . and your timing must be exactly right.

Get ready . . . soon now . . . not yet . . . not yet . . . NOW! Turn to PAGE 52!

You believe that you are dreaming, so when the earth beneath your feet begins to rumble and quake, you don't give it a second thought. After all, anything can happen in a dream. And you're sure that it is in the dream state that you'll find the Scarlet Sword. But then the rumbling grows worse. It gets so bad that you can no longer stand up. And when you fall, the invisible ground beneath your feet splits wide open, creating a huge crack that runs through the center of the island. And out of that dark pit a huge, six-fingered hand reaches out to grab you!

You laugh at the sight of the gigantic hand as it hovers in the air above you. "This is the silliest dream I've ever had," you chuckle.

But then it reaches down to pick you up off the ground. And you are not laughing anymore, Warrior. Six giant fingers wrap themselves around your body and then the hand descends back down into the dark pit.

It is time you realized you were not asleep. However, you are now—sleeping the sleep of the dead.

END

You sit down in the sand and ponder your problem. You know that the Wizard's magic will not bring you back to Silvergate. He told you that you would have to use the enchantment of the island. How, you wonder, can you harness its magic. You turn the Scarlet Sword in your hand and even try commanding it to take you home. But there is no magical response. There is only a familiar hungry growl. Once again you open your food pouch and this time leave the tiny animal the last of your cheese.

You close your eyes, trying desperately to find a way off this island. When you open them again, you find these words written in the sand: "Thank you for your gift of food. I repay your kindness by sending you . . ." And you see a furry little paw finish writing out the word *home*. In the next moment you're whisked away from the Island of Dreams, and the last thing you hear is a loud but friendly growl.

Turn to PAGE 26.

48

The giant eagles gently set you down in a swirling mist that seems to glow with all the colors of the rainbow.

"This is no ordinary mountain," says the Warrior as he pulls his Two-Handed Battle Sword from its scabbard.

"Indeed it is not," you answer softly, searching for the Demon's Lair. "It is in this that place we will find the Scarlet Sword. So said Merlin's Book of Life."

But in the multicolored haze it's difficult to see where you are going, and soon you find yourselves deep within a bubbling bog.

"We had better turn back and try another direction," you say at last.

The Warrior doesn't answer.

You look around. He's nowhere in sight!

"Where are you?" you shout. "Answer me!"

Silence—except for the sounds of the swamp, which grow louder and louder. Up to your waist in the bubbling muck, you turn back toward dry land to search for your friend. You take just two steps when something from the depths of the swamp grabs hold of your leg!

If you think it's the Warrior and try to help him, turn to PAGE 56.

If you think you'd better get out of this swamp now, turn to PAGE 61.

You hold the Scarlet Sword out in front of you and softly say, "The Warrior and I wish only to reunite you with the Scarlet Shield. If you take us back to the land from which we came, we will do our best to bring glory to your name and then return you and the shield to this sacred resting place. That is our oath."

Without any warning, the air within the Demon's Lair suddenly begins to circle you like a whirlpool. Behind you, you hear the shouts of the Warrior and turn to see him rushing into the cave with a tornado-like funnel cloud whirling at his heels.

"Do not run from it!" you cry out. "It is the magic of the Scarlet Sword—it will take us back to Silvergate!"

Or at least you hope so. . . .

The whirlwinds surround both of you. You are unable to see beyond this cocoon of driven air—until the whirling suddenly diminishes and you find yourself standing beside the Warrior in front of King Henry's castle!

And you've arrived not a moment too soon!

Beladar and his barbarian horde are gathering to make their final attack on the beleaguered kingdom. This time you are ready for them. Despite your earlier use of the Combat Magic, your magical journey home has somehow refreshed you. And, most important of all, you hold the Scarlet Sword of Shalimar in your hands as you stand in front of Silvergate ready to do battle.

Turn to PAGE 94, and be prepared for the fight of your life!

50

As you finish the chant the wind begins to howl, rising to a sound like a thousand wolves. Lightning cracks, filling the sky with the brightness of a thousand suns. And thunder peals, louder than a thousand soldiers' drums.

In the swirling clouds outside the open tower you see the image of a man. "I am Merlin," it speaks in a voice that seems to echo through the ages. "Why, Wizard, have you dared summon me from my rest?"

"If you are the mighty Merlin," you boldly reply, "and not the mere mirage of a storm, you would *know* why I have called you here."

The face in the clouds suddenly erupts with laughter, sending a rumbling through the valley below like the roar of a tidal wave.

"A *mirage . . . ?* You amuse me, Wizard," Merlin says, still smiling. "And, yes, I know why you have summoned me. In fact, I know more than I should. I have seen the day of your death written in the book of your life. Even this very meeting between us can be found there. And the answer to the question you seek—the way to defeat the Scarlet Shield of Shalimar—is written there as well." Merlin's voice becomes teasing. "I suggest you read page 64."

Don't delay! This is the Book of Life. Turn immediately to PAGE 64!

52

You reach out over the castle wall . . . and grab the flaming end of a red torch! Howling in pain, you stagger back, only to lose your footing and stumble off the parapet.

With a horrible crash, you hit the ground twelve feet below. Before you can get up, you're surrounded by a band of barbarians who bind your arms behind you and carry you away, a prisoner of war.

As they take you through the castle to the now-open gate, you see the ruins of Silvergate. Despite your efforts, King Henry's kingdom has fallen.

"Your King is dead, as are all his knights," sneers one of your captors. "Even the mighty Wizard lies slain with an arrow through his heart."

Would any of this have been different if you had left the castle when you had the chance and had somehow gotten the Scarlet Shield of Shalimar away from Beladar?

It does you no good to wonder about such things. What matters is that you're alive. And though chains now bind you, you vow that you will not give up life until Beladar has paid for what he has done this night!

Go on to PAGE 53.

The barbarians drop you in a dirty hut at the outskirts of their camp. Though they killed everyone else who fought for Silvergate, for some reason they have saved you. Why?

You soon discover the answer when Beladar, the Scarlet Shield on his arm, marches into the hut and stares down at you. From your position on the ground, he looks almost twice as tall as his awesome seven-foot stature.

"So you are the soldier who fought so bravely. My men told me that you even tried to hold fire in your hands. Is that true?"

"It wasn't fire I was trying to hold," you admit, "but what I thought was your Scarlet Shield."

"You will make a worthy sacrifice," he says with an evil smile. "My army will gain strength from the courage that we squeeze out of your soul."

Beladar calls in two of his soldiers, who untie you and hold you by your arms.

"Take him to the center of the camp," orders Beladar, "and then let the torture begin!"

This is your only chance. With just two soldiers holding your arms, it's now or never. . . .

Turn to **PAGE 91**.

54

You draw your blade and swoop down to meet this bird of horror in battle.

One of the vulture's heads tries to rip off your right arm, while the other head tries to take a piece out of your left leg. Before it can do its bloody work, you bring your blade down with all your strength and lop off one of its heads!

Instead of blood, from out of the wound come small white doves. And as more of the beautiful birds fly out of the vulture's body, the monster itself begins to wither and die. You shake your head, unsure if what you see is reality or illusion.

The vulture drops like a stone into the waters below. And you fly down after it, exhausted from your battle, wondering what other evil enchantments await you on the Island of Dreams.

Turn to PAGE 13.

The dragon raises its head to take a deep breath. You know that your life may be over in the next chilling moment. But in your dream you are sure you have the one weapon that might save you: the Whistling Mace.

Weird things can happen in dreams. Will your Whistling Mace be there when you reach for it? There is only way to find out: Flip a coin high up into the air—at least three feet over your head.

If you catch it, turn to PAGE 59.

If you don't catch the coin, turn to PAGE 12.

56

You reach down into the bog and take hold of something green and slimy. The Warrior must be totally covered with muck, you think to yourself as you try to lift him out of the depths.

But it isn't the Warrior at all!

Bursting from beneath the surface of the swamp, held in your own hands, is a creature with the huge head of a rat and the tentacles of an octopus!

It wraps its eight long arms around you and drags you down into the bog. There, beneath the surface, the jaws of the monster open and devour you.

In the end you make a very tasty meal. (Wizards, after all, are a great delicacy.) And now that you've been a demon's dinner, you can chew on all the things you might have done differently—*that* should give you plenty of food for thought. In the meantime, close the book and open it again only when you're hungry for a new adventure in the land of *Wizards, Warriors, and You.*

END

As you throw the Flying Spear, a blade of red light from the Scarlet Shield cuts through the air. Only seconds later, before your spear has found its mark, the red light of the Scarlet Shield slices through your armor.

As you topple to the ground, dead, your Flying Spear soars across the battlefield . . . and it sails over the top of the Scarlet Shield, striking Beladar right between the eyes!

You've killed him!

But you haven't saved the kingdom. Another barbarian quickly picks up the Scarlet Shield of Shalimar and now *he* has the power of Merlin's creation. You, Warrior, have died for nothing. And, to add insult to injury, your enchanted spear never even came back. Some days nothing goes right.

END

58

To conjure up the spirit of Merlin seems like an impossible task. But these are desperate times. Merlin, the ancient sorcerer who created the Scarlet Shield, is the only soul—alive or dead—who can tell you how to overcome its power.

With an owl's feather in your left hand and a lighted candle made from the fat of a wild boar in your right, you head for the top of the northern tower. Here, alone on the cold, windswept heights, you thrice chant the magic words that must reach across a world of time and pierce the dark barrier of death itself. . . .

Turn to PAGE 50.

The Whistling Mace is right where you left it. You grab for it, whirl it around, and then send it flying straight and true toward the head of the dragon. But before it can hit its target, the dragon releases a burst of arctic breath and freezes the mace in a block of ice. It drops heavily to the ground and whistles no more.

Desperate, you reach for the Sword of the Golden Lion, but your scabbard is empty. The sword has vanished! You need another weapon—any weapon! On the ground is a long stick with a pointed edge. You pick it up and start to throw it at the dragon. But that's as far as you get. As you throw the makeshift lance you slip on a patch of ice and fall onto the long, pointed pole.

And with the dragon's next breath you are turned into a new dessert treat: Frozen Warrior on a Stick.

END

60

There is neither good nor evil in an object; it merely serves its holder. And so it is with the Scarlet Shield of Shalimar. . . .

Just as you invoke the spell of Sorcerer's Sleep, Beladar's left arm rises, and with it the shield that protects him. It glows a shimmering red, becoming a smooth scarlet-tinted mirror—and reflecting your spell directly back at you!

Both you and the Warrior instantly collapse into deep, untroubled sleep.

Hours later you wake to the smell of something burning—*you!* Beladar is roasting both you and the Warrior over a roaring fire. Rest assured, before his evil work is through, you'll be well done. Which is more than can be said for your mission. . . .

END

You try to pull away from whatever is holding you, but the grip cannot be broken. Then you feel something wrap itself around your other leg.

You can't move!

And now, beneath your feet, the swamp begins to open up as if you were standing in quicksand. You slowly sink down, down, down into the bog.

As the murky water rises to your chest you prepare to cast a spell.

The green, slimy liquid begins to lap at your throat. . . .

You're halfway through the chant that will set your spell in motion.

The bubbling bog seeps up over your mouth just as you are about to complete the spell. . . .

It's too late now, Wizard! As if a trap door has been opened, you suddenly disappear from the surface of the bog.

Turn to **PAGE 71**.

62

The Scarlet Sword sends a thick cloud of red dust into the air that chokes the front ranks of the enemy soldiers. But this is an army that has never lost under the leadership of Beladar, and he urges them on. . . .

The fierce invaders from the north surge forward again, and even the Scarlet Sword has trouble stopping them all. It brings down upon them red hail the size of a man's fist, then crimson sparks that explode like thunder. Yet they keep on coming.

The Warrior, also strengthened by the magical journey, is swinging the Whistling Mace, slaying barbarians by the hundreds. Still, you realize that the two of you—even with the Scarlet Sword—cannot wipe out an entire army. You must chop off its head to truly kill it—and that means you must battle Beladar and the Scarlet Shield!

But as you cut your way through the enemy lines, the flying forest, which you chose not to fight, slams into the castle gates, smashing them apart. A huge gaping hole now exists for Beladar's hordes to rush through. Should you stay with the Warrior to keep the enemy out or should you continue to search for Beladar in the hope that you can defeat him?

If you stay behind to defend the castle, turn to PAGE 8.

If you go on to search for Beladar, turn to PAGE 84.

As you turn toward the moat, the Scarlet Shield's magic creates a boulder the size of the castle's western tower. It hovers in the air for a moment and then hurtles toward you, as if it had been launched by a catapult.

Though it may may not look very heroic, you jump back into the moat. And it's wise that you do, because the boulder rips through the air where you were just standing and smashes into the base of the castle wall, making a huge hole.

Instantly, the water from the moat rushes into the castle, and you find yourself washed up into the courtyard. Feeling very wet and a little silly, you look up. And there stands the Wizard with a deeply troubled look on his face.

Turn to PAGE 28.

64

And it is written:

Let it be known that the Scarlet Sword is the only weapon on earth that equals the Scarlet Shield. The sword and the shield were buried at the foot of the Demon's Lair in a place called Shalimar. It is to this place that good and evil shall be drawn—and there they shall do battle for the fate of humanity.

The Scarlet Shield will defend he who holds it from force of arms and feats of sorcery, while the Scarlet Sword holds within its enchanted steel the power of a thousand wondrous spells.

To defeat Beladar, you need to find the Scarlet Sword. You and the Warrior must venture to Shalimar at once! Hurry and turn to PAGE 19.

You and the Warrior are soaring over the peak of Mount Shalimar. You've made it! Slowly, you begin the chant to decrease the powers of the spell.

But the spell doesn't break!

Frantically, you use every bit of sorcery you can think of to try to stop the gales, but it's impossible. Trapped by the wild power of your own magic, you fly past Shalimar, past the kingdoms beyond, out over the seas, and you're blown into the eternal unknown—lost forever upon the winds of time. . . .

END

What is it that comes crawling out of the shadows? It's the Warrior! And he's hurt. His armor is badly dented and his Two-Handed Battle Sword is broken in half.

You rush to him, but he waves you away. "There," he says weakly, pointing into the darkness, "is the Demon's Lair." He stops to catch his breath and glances down at his broken sword. "I saw the spot from where Beladar stole the Scarlet Shield. The ground was covered with blood. He must have barely escaped with his life. But the creature within," he says, gesturing toward the cave, "will not let that happen again. It brought us down here to die. . . . It means to kill us both."

"What it *means* to do and what it *will* do are two different things," you say.

"Indeed they are," the Warrior says, grinning in spite of his obvious pain. "And together we will triumph over demon and barbarian!" He casts aside his broken blade and pulls from his belt the deadly Bludgeon. On wobbly legs the Warrior rises to his feet. "Let us venture back to the Demon's Lair and show the monster who awaits us the true meaning of the word *valor*!"

Turn to PAGE 80.

You fly upward, drawing the Bludgeon from your side and hoping you won't have to use it. But the vulture follows swiftly. With a terrifying shriek, it closes in. You struggle in the air, using the Bludgeon to fend off its furious attacks. But no matter how skillfully you use your weapon, there seems to be no escape from the razor-sharp beaks.

Finally, you manage to strike one of its heads, and the bird seems dazed for a moment. Without waiting to see how seriously you've hurt it, you propel yourself toward the island. You're almost there! Then, just as you're sure you've lost the vulture, you feel twelve armor-piercing talons sink into your back. You wriggle there helplessly, unable to break free.

The winged fiend slowly drifts toward the island in lazy circles while your blood drips down to the water below. By the time the vulture lands, your life has ended. And it's probably a good thing, because the bird has brought you back to its nest to feed its young. Little two-headed vultures love the taste of warriors.

END

68

You wait until the flying forest is directly over the charging army of invaders, and then you lift the Scarlet Sword of Shalimar and point it at the trees.

"Change these mighty oaks into splinters of death," you command, "and cast them down upon the enemy!"

The blue sky turns red and the flying forest *explodes* in midflight. The huge tree trunks are shattered into ten thousand sharp-edged pieces. Like spears, arrows, and daggers, they come plunging down in a murderous volley that no army on earth could survive.

Deadly slivers of wood rain down on Beladar's soldiers in a slashing, cutting storm of death. They can find no escape from the power of the Scarlet Sword.

In one display of its magnificent magic, the sword has almost completely destroyed the enemy. The battlefield is littered with bodies and blood. But your real foe is not the invading army—it is Beladar and the Scarlet Shield.

And now, with vengeance burning in his eyes, Beladar comes to slay you.

Go on to PAGE 70.

70

The Scarlet Shield protected Beladar from the deadly rain you sent down upon his men, and he is now determined that nothing protect *you!*

With his tremendous strength, animal cunning, and the powerful magic within the Scarlet Shield, he comes to seize the Scarlet Sword from you in what you both know will be a combat to the death!

Every dangerous choice you've made has led to this moment. Turn to PAGE 83 . . . and good luck!

It seems like a miracle but, though you were pulled deep beneath the surface of the slime, you haven't drowned. In fact, you were quickly pulled right *through* the slimy water into a dry cavern set in an air pocket underneath the bog. But who—or what— brought you here?

On the far side of the cave, deep in shadow, a figure stirs. It seems to creep toward you in the darkness, and you ready yourself for the worst.

You step back a few paces until your heels touch a stone wall. There is no place for you to hide. Whatever demon brought you here must have magic at least as powerful as your own. And it's crawling across the floor, coming right at you. Still hidden by the deep shadows, it inches toward you.

"Come no farther!" you declare.

It ignores you.

"You may slay me," you proclaim, "but by all that is holy, I vow that I'll not die alone. Your blood will fill this cavern along with mine!"

Out of the shadows it comes for you. . . .

Turn to PAGE 66.

72

You hold your cloak out at your sides, as if it were wings, and silently invoke the spell of Flight. Then, without warning, you suddenly rise up off the ground and fly directly at Beladar! The barbarian starts to raise the Scarlet Shield . . . but he's too slow. You grab the shield from his hands and soar straight up into the clouds.

You've done it!

But down below is the Warrior, left to fight the entire army of barbarians alone. You can't leave him to die. Helping your friend should be easy enough, you reason. After all, you now possess the Scarlet Shield of Shalimar!

Turn to PAGE 81.

When your vision clears, your hands are empty. The Scarlet Sword has disappeared! In fact, far more than the sword has vanished. Two full days of your life are gone; it is as if you never lived them. And, most incredible of all, you do not even realize it!

None of what you have just gone through remains in your memory. It has all been wiped away by the perverse magic of the Scarlet Sword. You are destined to live these last two days all over again—but there's no telling how they will turn out . . . because history rarely repeats itself in the world of *Wizards, Warriors, and You.*

Turn back to PAGE 5 and prepare to make new choices!

"Show me the true Scarlet Shield," you tell the sword. It responds by pointing at the far right image of Beladar.

Now you know your real enemy. Suddenly, all six images of your foe raise long leather whips. You ignore the other five and attack the real Beladar, stabbing him in the leg and forcing him to lower the shield. Immediately, you thrust the Scarlet Sword deep into his chest.

You can hardly believe you've won such a quick and easy victory. And you're right—it isn't a victory at all. . . .

The five phantom Beladars do not disappear with the death of their master. Rather, they continue the attack. Two whips wrap around your legs and pull you to the ground. Two more whips wrap around your shoulders, pinning your arms to your sides. And the fifth whip curls around the Scarlet Sword and pulls it out of your hand.

This last phantom Beladar takes hold of the sword and quickly uses it to kill the other four illusions. Then the seven-foot phantom looks down at you on the ground. "I may not be flesh and blood," it says, "but I possess the Scarlet Shield and now the Scarlet Sword. And with this power, the first thing I will do is give myself life. The second thing I will do, Warrior, is give you your death!"

Tangled in the whips, you cannot move as the blade of the Scarlet Sword slashes down across your neck.

END

Beladar doesn't bother calling upon the magic of the Scarlet Shield. He is sure that, because of your weakened state, he can send you into the arms of death without magic. And with a hard, slashing blow of his cutlass that nearly hacks off your right arm, he just might be right.

Beladar is fast for such a giant of a man. And it doesn't help you to have a spear sticking out of your shoulder. But that gives you an idea. . . .

Pretending to stumble backwards, you suddenly yank the spear out of your body and throw it at Beladar! The incredible pain you suffer is worth the look of surprise on the huge barbarians's face as the spear is about to strike.

But then, seemingly of its own will, the Scarlet Shield jumps up to protect its master. Your spear bounces harmlessly off its jewel-encrusted surface. Before the angry Beladar can lunge at you with his cutlass, you rob the barbarian of his rage by suddenly collapsing. There, with the Scarlet Shield so teasingly close, you die from loss of blood.

Close the book. You have fought well and died well. No more than that can be asked of any warrior. Your show of courage has earned you the right to reenter the world of *Wizards, Warriors, and You* at any time you wish. That is, of course, if all your courage hasn't already been bled out of you.

END

76

With the Sword of the Golden Lion held high, you take just one step before the entire tent is bathed in a brilliant crimson light. You stand there frozen, unable to move. *You've been turned to stone!*

Time passes. Months . . . years . . . centuries . . . and now pigeons sit on your mighty arm, and on summer days people come and eat their lunches at your feet.

You've become a statue in a park!

And though the landscape around you has changed, with each century one thing remains constant. Throughout the years everyone who passes marvels at your lifelike appearance. There is even a myth that has come to be told about you—that once, long ago, you were a man of flesh and blood who was turned to stone by the magic of an enchanted shield. But, of course, no one believes that silly story.

END

As the spell of Invisibility quickly comes to your aid, you realize that you've called upon the wrong spell. It may be that Beladar can't see you, but fire has no eyes. The flames of the Scarlet Shield engulf you, blazing across your cloak and robes. And because you are invisible, it appears as if the flames have a life of their own as you race toward the cold water of the castle moat.

You've long since dropped the Scarlet Sword, and Beladar picks it up from the ground as he watches what looks like a running fire leap into the moat.

You stay submerged for what feels like hours. You've become visible again by the time you rise to the water's surface. And there, waiting, stands Beladar—but not to give you a helping hand. Before you can cast a spell for your own protection, Beladar uses the magic that is now his—and ends your life with the Scarlet Sword.

END

78

As you complete the words of the Shrink spell the huge stones hurled at you become nothing more than pebbles . . . and the creature that threw them is reduced to the size of a small dog. A very angry small dog. Its speed surprises you and you are unprepared for the running leap it makes as it tries to rip out your throat with its teeth.

You fall backward, but the creature holds onto you by grabbing you by the hair with five of its hands. You swing your head around so that you smash the tenacious demon into a wall, and it finally lets go.

This time you pick up a large rock and get ready to drop it on the stunned little monster. But the demon is too fast. It sees you and hurries out of your range, out of the cave toward the Warrior, who waits out beyond the darkness.

Turn to PAGE 23.

Not a single barbarian remains in the Warrior's way, and his journey back to Silvergate is swift. In the throne room he presents King Henry the prize of the quest: the Scarlet Shield of Shalimar.

The King beams with pleasure. But then a sadness overtakes him. "What of our dear friend, the Wizard?" he asks.

The Warrior bows his head. "I know not. I never saw him again after he entered the tent. I fear he was slain by the evil Beladar."

King Henry sighs. "It is too costly a victory, then." Eyes downcast, he reaches for the shield. But before he can touch it the Scarlet Shield explodes in a cloud of red smoke. When the vapors finally clear, the shield is gone and you find yourself facing an open-mouthed King Henry.

"You are safe!" exclaims the Warrior with a cry of joy.

"Yes," you reply, "but I am afraid we have failed the King and all our people."

"No one has failed yet," the King says, putting an arm around your shoulder. "As long as we breathe there is hope. There is still time, Wizard."

"Perhaps," you reply without conviction, "but not much. I must quickly find the secret to defeating the power of the shield—and there is only one who can help me . . . Merlin!"

Turn to PAGE 58.

80

You take the Warrior by the arm and gently tell him, "Your spirit is great, but your strength is as broken as your blade. Rest, my friend, while I face this demon and trick it out toward you. By then you will have regained some of your strength and will be ready to do battle."

Fearing for your safety, the Warrior at first refuses. Finally, though with great reluctance, he agrees. "I will do as you ask," he says, "on one condition."

"And that is?"

"If neither you nor the demon come out of the lair before the count of thirty, I am coming in after you. And nothing will stop me."

You smile at your companion, well aware that even magic could not change his mind. "It is agreed," you say.

Just the same, both of you know that by the count of thirty the monster could kill you one hundred times over. And knowing that this may be the last action of your life, you slowly walk into the unknown horror of the Demon's Lair. . . .

The creature awaits you on PAGE 6. Turn there if you dare!

You swoop back down over Beladar's camp and point the Scarlet Shield at the ring of barbarians closing in on the Warrior. A bright red light, like a giant bloody saber, cuts a path of escape through the enemy lines.

But it is only a beginning. A horde of soldiers fills the bloody opening, and you must yet again call upon the power of the shield. This second blast of blazing red light from Merlin's ancient creation scatters the enemy and gives the Warrior a chance to get away. One more taste of the shield's powerful magic will surely send the barbarians into full retreat!

You turn and glide up toward the clouds, positioning the shield for the final attack. But then, just as you are about to unleash its power on Beladar's troops for the last time, the Flight spell suddenly ends! You're nearly a mile high in the sky when you begin to fall like a rock. . . .

As you tumble head over heels through the air the Scarlet Shield of Shalimar slips out of your hands— and lands undamaged right at Beladar's feet. You also land at Beladar's feet. But you are very damaged—as in dead!

Close the book, Wizard. There'll be no more flying for you until you are ready to once again take off into the world of *Wizards, Warriors, and You.*

END

You are about to command the Scarlet Sword to create five duplicate Warriors, but before you can utter the words, one of the Beladars attacks with a hooked dagger. You sidestep his thrust, running him through with your sword. At the touch of your blade, he disintegrates. Another Beladar lunges at you with an axe. You use your sword to block the blow meant to crush your skull and then grab this image of Beladar and throw him over your shoulder. When he hits the ground, the Scarlet Shield in his hands goes flying—and this Beladar as well as his shield vaporize into thin air.

The battle continues. You destroy yet another phantom Beladar—and then another . . . until you look around and see that all of the illusions are gone.

There are just the two of you left.

Beladar carries a deadly broadsword and his Scarlet Shield. You have only the Scarlet Sword . . . and your skill.

Suddenly Beladar swings his broadsword and you duck under the slashing blade. You counter with a thrust meant for his throat, but he raises his shield. And at that moment, when your Scarlet Sword clangs against his Scarlet Shield, both magical weapons simply disappear!

Merlin created the two weapons as a matched set—for one to touch the other in mortal combat is to send them both instantly back to their sacred burial place.

But now you have no weapon at all—and Beladar is charging toward you with his broadsword!

Think fast and turn to PAGE 86.

Beladar carries a spiked club and the Scarlet Shield. But there are two of you, and that should give you an advantage. The Warrior holds the Sword of the Golden Lion and you wield the Scarlet Sword of Shalimar.

Though he's outnumbered, Beladar boldly attacks, rushing straight at you with his club. The Warrior tries to help you by jumping in front of the barbarian, but Beladar never intended using the club. Instead, he smashes the Scarlet Shield against the side of the Warrior's head, and your friend falls unconscious to the ground.

Now, without the Warrior beside you, the odds are suddenly in Beladar's favor. He has both his club, a mortal weapon, and the immortal Scarlet Shield. Will the Scarlet Sword alone be enough to save you?

You'll know soon enough. . . .

Turn to PAGE 90.

84

The Scarlet Sword is covered with the blood of more than three thousand enemy soldiers—and still you cannot find Beladar. It is as if he has disappeared.

Behind you, you hear the war cries of the barbarians as they finally defeat the heroic Warrior and leave him for dead with a lance through his heart. Your friend has given his life in the desperate hope that the kingdom might be saved. And, as you look back, you see that King Henry's castle is being overrun. Of all the defenders of Silvergate, you alone are left on the battlefield. The war is lost. Beladar, wherever he is, has wisely avoided you and won his prize. Any victory you might win against him now would mean nothing to those whom you failed to save.

Yet the Scarlet Sword is still in your hands, and it possesses a magic so strong that it might even now help you turn defeat into victory.

"Great Sword," you softly utter, "by the power that Merlin cast into your steel blade, take me back in time so that I might redeem my past mistakes. Give me another chance to save the kingdom and my friend the Warrior, so that those I have failed might live again."

The Scarlet Sword has the power to grant you your wish. But how far back in time will it take you? Pick a number from one to ten.

If you've chosen an odd number, turn to PAGE 94.

If you've chosen an even number, turn to PAGE 11.

You fight fire with fire!

The blaze from the spell of Merlin's Fire bursts from the fingertips of your left hand, blocking the flames coming at you from the Scarlet Shield. And with your right hand you swing the Scarlet Sword at Beladar's head.

Beladar dodges your blow, but now he knows he's in a fight to the death. With his mighty club, he tries to smash your left hand, to stop your fiery spell. You pull back a step, and his club flies through the flames, turning the heavy wooden weapon into a blazing torch.

Now Beladar has two flaming weapons instead of one. But not for long. With a thrust and parry that would make the Warrior proud, you lash out and slice Beladar's burning club off at the handle!

Startled by your bold maneuver, Beladar's concentration is broken, and the flames suddenly stop shooting out of his shield. But *your* spell is still in force, and Merlin's Fire leaps onto the Scarlet Shield.

Though the shield glows from the heat, it does not burn. It *cannot* burn. Beladar laughs. Taunting, he cries out, "Your puny efforts are wasted. This magic of yours is nothing compared to that of my shield. But I've toyed with you long enough, Wizard. Now you will die!"

Turn to PAGE 87.

86

Beladar swings his blade and draws blood, slashing a wound in your right arm.

You keep backing up as he relentlessly pursues you.

Your arm is bleeding badly. And then Beladar makes a sudden move to his right and cuts a deep wound in your other arm!

It's almost as if he is toying with you. In fact, Beladar is smiling now, sure that you're as good as dead. He finally moves in for the kill, thrusting his broadsword right at your belly. . . .

Though your arms are wounded, there is nothing wrong with your legs. You kick the sword out of his hand and it goes flying high into the air. But now you've left yourself off balance, and Beladar grabs you in a bone-crunching bear hug. He lifts you off the ground and squeezes, trying to break your back. You can feel your ribs cracking under the pressure—but then it suddenly stops! The sword you kicked out of his hands has finally come down out of the sky . . . and found its home in the top of Beladar's head! He topples over, dead!

Return to Silvergate for a hero's welcome on PAGE 88!

While Beladar was boasting, you continued to keep Merlin's Fire burning on the Scarlet Shield. You've been waiting for something to happen. . . .

And then it does: The shield gets so hot from the flame that Beladar can no longer hold it. With a scream that shakes the very ground, the giant barbarian suddenly drops the Scarlet Shield!

With no army, no club, and finally no magic shield to protect Beladar, you put the sharp point of the Scarlet Sword up against his throat.

"Please!" he begs. "Let me live!"

"It is up to King Henry to decide your fate," you tell the sniveling barbarian.

Just then, you hear the Warrior groan. Gently, you help your gallant friend to his feet.

"I fear I was of little help," admits the Warrior, "but I am glad to see this happy outcome upon awakening."

"You took the blow that was meant for me," you remind him, "and nearly sacrificed your life so that I might live. And for this you apologize? No," you tell your friend, "we are a team. And we win or lose as a team. I could not have reached this moment without you."

The two of you clasp hands, and then take your vanquished foe through the opening castle gates. . . .

A grateful kingdom awaits you on PAGE 95.

When you walk through the gate into the castle's courtyard, the Wizard leads a great crowd of cheering citizens.

"I knew you could do it!" your friend declares. "And I am proud of you. You saved the kingdom."

"*We* saved the kingdom," you correct him. "I could never have gotten the Scarlet Sword without you."

"But you fought Beladar all alone," counters the Wizard.

"Perhaps, but you—"

"What? Is this a meeting of the Modesty Society?" laughs King Henry as he puts his arm around your shoulder. "Soon you'll be saying it is I who deserve all the credit for defeating Beladar!"

"We fought in your name," you instantly reply.

"That, indeed, makes the victory yours, sire," adds the Wizard.

"Nonsense," says King Henry. "Your names will live through all time because of what you did this day."

And the King is right. In fact, many stories will someday be written about how you defeated the Scarlet Shield of Shalimar and saved the kingdom. But this will be the only story that tells the truth!

END

Your eyes bulge out of their sockets as Beladar's massive hand tightens around your throat. You'd cry out, but you haven't the breath; you'd fight back, but you haven't the strength; you'd cast a spell, but you haven't the time—because with one last squeeze of his mighty hand, Beladar sends you into the impenetrable darkness known as death!

You must exist in this bleak realm until you once more have the courage to enter the world of *Wizards, Warriors, and You*. Only then will you be free to continue your quest for the Scarlet Shield of Shalimar!

END

Beladar swings his club at you and nearly imbeds its spike in the top of your head. Only at the last instant do you leap out of the way. But not quite far enough. The spike rips a deep wound along your arm—the arm that holds the Scarlet Sword. When you try to change hands, Beladar lunges forward with the Scarlet Shield and knocks you off balance.

Now Beladar has you where he wants you. With your arm too weak to wield the sword, you are completely defenseless—or so it appears—and he commands the Scarlet Shield to set you on fire!

A wave of flame shoots out from the jewels on the Scarlet Shield. But you have protection that Beladar can't see. You have the powers of your own sorcery!

One spell, and one spell only, will save you. If you think your salvation lies with Spell #10, Merlin's Fire, turn to PAGE 85.

If you think your way to victory lies with Spell #4, Invisibility, turn to PAGE 77.

Only a master of the fighting arts would even attempt what you do next. You dive into a somersault, taking the two barbarians with you as you barrel right into the stunned Beladar. The shock of the collision sends the two soldiers flying and knocks Beladar out of the tent.

As fast as a heartbeat, you grab one of the fallen soldiers' swords. And if you are quick enough, you might just be able to overcome the barbarian leader before he recovers and uses the Scarlet Shield's magic to destroy you.

Speed is everything. Pick a number, odd or even.
If you chose odd, turn to **PAGE 76**.
If you chose even, turn to **PAGE 93**.

Outside the throne room the Warrior turns to you. "Beladar and his horde may well overrun Silvergate before we return," he says anxiously. "Which spell will you cast to take us to Mount Shalimar?"

Which spell indeed? If you use the spell to Command Animals, you could summon one of the creatures of the sky to bring you to Shalimar. Then again, you've known a few animals who've simply refused to obey the spell's command, and this is no time to have to fuss with a stubborn bird.

You could also summon The Wind to carry you, but The Wind can be as unpredictable as any animal.

If you choose Spell #6, Command Animals, turn to PAGE 30.

If you choose Spell # 8, The Wind, turn to PAGE 37.

You race out of the tent to find Beladar waiting for you. He holds the shield before him, and all looks lost.

What can you do with a sword at twenty paces?

Nothing—at least that is what the barbarian leader thinks. You see a glint of laughter in his eyes, and that's when you throw your sword. Like a huge dagger, it hurtles end over end toward Beladar's head. The sword is only inches from Beladar when a bolt of lightning shoots out of the Scarlet Shield and strikes the flying blade—*and turns it completely around!*

Your own sword is coming at you now, and you have no shield for protection. You have only your brave heart . . . which sadly becomes the blade's resting place.

END

94

A mighty cheer goes up from the castle walls behind you as King Henry and the citizens of the kingdom rejoice at your return. But ahead of you there is no cheering. There is only the vast invading army of Beladar. And the gigantic leader of the barbarians is marching forward, the Scarlet Shield of Shalimar held firmly in his hands.

At Beladar's command, the shield's magic rips towering trees out of the nearby forest and sends them hurtling toward the castle's front gates like huge spears. At the same time, the barbarian army charges the castle walls!

Should you direct the Scarlet Sword to fight the barbarians or the flying forest? Your decision could mean the difference between victory and defeat. Choose and discover your destiny!

If you decide to fight the barbarians first, turn to PAGE 62.

If your first decision is to defend yourself against the flying forest, turn to PAGE 68.

You and the Warrior enter Silvergate to the wild cheers of the citizenry. With flowers being thrown down upon you from the parapets, you march ahead with your prisoner.

Before King Henry passes sentence upon the brutal invader, he stands before the assembled knights and ladies of the court and proclaims, "I speak for all the people of this kingdom when I say that both the Wizard and the Warrior will forever be in our hearts. And in their future quests, may that gratitude and love strengthen them."

"Thank you, My Lord," you humbly reply for both the Warrior and yourself. "Your kind words have touched our souls."

"Speaking of souls," adds the Warrior, "what would you have us do with Beladar?"

The King ponders this for a moment and then smiles at the barbarian. "You have always been the hawk, Beladar. It is time you learned what it is to be the dove. My sentence is that the Wizard shall use his powers to turn you into a little white dove so that you may learn the meaning of fear."

Later, after the frightened dove takes to the skies, you and the Warrior return the Scarlet Shield and the Scarlet Sword to their resting place.

And as for you, Wizard, you brought peace to King Henry's kingdom—and a legacy of glory unto yourself. And so it is written in your Book of Life.

END

The Book of Spells

For use only by the WIZARD

As the Wizard, you may use any of these powerful spells. But remember, magic is mysterious and unpredictable. Use it wisely.

Spell #1: Move Time Forward

This spell allows you to move time forward. The spell can move time forward one hour at the most. It can sometimes be very useful for getting out of tight situations. But it's a dangerous spell to use, since the future is often unpredictable, and surprises may await you there.

Spell #2: Forest Imp's Freeze

Named after a lowly forest imp who accidentally discovered it, this spell allows you to freeze anyone in his or her tracks. The spell will work on one person or many, but they must be in view. The victims will not be able to move a muscle for the length of the spell — but they will be awake and able to see and hear your actions. You must move quickly. The spell lasts a very short time.

Spell #3: Conjurer's Confusion

A simple but effective spell. When cast, it throws the mind of a foe into total confusion. It can be used on only one person at a time. Its major drawback is that you cannot predict how long the spell will last. And if there are any mirrors or reflecting objects in sight, the confusion could reflect onto the spellcaster!

Spell #4: Invisibility

A basic spell known even by apprentice sorcerers, you can use it to become instantly and completely invisible.

A useful spell for fast escapes from desperate situations, it has one major drawback: You cannot predict how long the invisibility will last. It could last for several weeks — or a few seconds.

This spell can also be used to make an enemy or a friend invisible.

Spell #5: Sorcerer's Sleep

This spell can be used to put anyone standing within 100 feet of you to sleep immediately. The spell can work on one person or on an entire army of people. Unfortunately, the length of time the victims will sleep cannot be predicted. It may be just for a few seconds, or for days. Another drawback: If the spell is incorrectly cast, it can put the spellcaster to sleep instead of its intended target.

Spell #6: Command Animals

This difficult spell gives you the power to speak to animals and command them to do your bidding. It is an unpredictable spell since animals have strong wills that sometimes cannot be swayed by magic. Occasionally, animals will choose to disobey your commands. From time to time, the spell causes friendly animals to become hostile.

Spell #7: Shift Shape

This spell causes you to change shape — to assume the appearance of an animal, plant, or any object that is *within view.* The spell can also be used to change the appearance of others. The spell lasts for only a few minutes. It wears off suddenly, returning the subject to his or her original appearance.

Spell #8: The Wind

This spell conjures up a hurricane-force wind, strong enough to blow away the toughest foe. A dangerous spell, it must be used with utmost care — for once the wind has been summoned, it cannot be controlled! It may turn against the spellcaster despite all efforts to turn it around.

Spell #9: Flight

This spell allows you to fly. It can also be used to make others fly. If conjured correctly, it will allow you to fly above trees for a distance as far as 100 miles. A dangerous and exhausting spell, it can be used only once per adventure. Warning: If the spell is incorrectly cast, you may lose the power of flight in midair!

Spell #10: Merlin's Fire

This spell can be used to start a blazing fire on any object. It cannot be used on people or animals. The fire burns with intensity and cannot be extinguished until the spell is removed. This is a dangerous spell because the fire can spread out of control within seconds if the wind should change direction.

(*Note:* This spell is named for Merlin but there is no known account of his having used it.)

Spell #11: Shrink

This spell causes a foe or foes to shrink in size. Its effect is immediate and can be used on anyone — or anything — within 100 yards. As with other spells, it is impossible to predict exactly how small someone will become or how long he or she will stay that way.

Spell #12: Combat Magic

This spell allows you to combat a magic spell that has been used against you or against a companion. It will immediately dispel any magic, except that of a Grand Wizard. This spell requires such concentration and energy that after performing it the spellcaster must rest for one entire day. *The spell can be used only once during an adventure.*

**Now that you have studied your spells,
begin your adventure on page 11.**

The Book of Weapons

For use only by the WARRIOR

As the Warrior, you may use all the weapons listed here. But remember, a great warrior uses wisdom as well as might.

Weapon #1: The Sword of the Golden Lion

You won this sword in a battle to the death against the Lancashire Sorcerer, and it has been at your side ever since. The blade bears a lion, etched in gold. The scabbard carries the inscription *Forever*, because the sword is an immortal weapon that cannot be broken. It is said that your sword was created by the same swordsmith who forged the legendary Excalibur.

YOU CARRY THE SWORD OF THE GOLDEN LION AT ALL TIMES. IN ADDITION, YOU MAY ARM YOURSELF WITH THREE OTHER WEAPONS FROM THE FOLLOWING LIST.

Weapon #2: Two-Handed Battle Sword

This long, heavy sword requires two hands to swing. But its weight and the sharpness of its inch-thick blade enable it to cut through armor. A single swing of this awesome weapon is usually enough to devastate a foe.

Weapon #3: The Cutlass of Cornwall

This small, curved sword is efficient for fighting in close quarters. Originally owned by the Cornwall Conjurer, the cutlass is said to have magical abilities that allow it to keep fighting an opponent after its owner has fallen. Dark legends about the cutlass say that it has been known to turn unpredictably on its owner!

Weapon #4: Triple Crossbow

Designed especially for you by the Wizard, this crossbow is small and easy to carry. But it can propel three arrows at once in different directions. This makes it especially effective when fighting alone against many.

Weapon #5: Bludgeon

A short pole for a handle that ends in a weighted tip with jutting, iron spikes all around it, this weapon is unsophisticated but effective. The bludgeon isn't much good against armor, but it can deliver a powerful head wound.

Weapon #6: Flail

Used for whipping or choking, this is a weapon for desperate situations. It consists of a short, wooden pole attached by a cord to a long, wooden handle. Many knights find this weapon unchivalrous; but sometimes a warrior must use even the cruelest tools of his trade.

Weapon #7: Whistling Mace

A long mace with a diamond-shaped, many-faceted blade on the end, this weapon whistles when you swing it. Legend has it that an enchantress is trapped within the blade and sings as she guides it to its destination. You use the mace as a spear or as a lance. Whether or not it truly is enchanted, it is deadly accurate.

Weapon #8: Devil's Dagger

The dagger resembles a small sword except that the blade is thinner and shorter. The dagger is worn on the side opposite the sword, and is usually used to deliver a death blow to someone who has already fallen. Your dagger is called the Devil's Dagger because of your superhuman skill at using it.

Weapon #9: Flying Spear

This silver spear, enchanted by the Wizard, can be thrown five times farther than a normal spear — and it will then fly back to your hand. A weapon that has been known to shock and terrify entire armies, it must be thrown accurately, or it could possibly fly back at you with unfortunate results.

**Now that you are suitably armed for your quest,
you may begin your adventure on page 17.**

About the Authors

Barbara Siegel and Scott Siegel are the authors of 20 books. The majority of their work has been for young adults, writing novels in categories such as horror, fantasy and adventure, as well as nonfiction books on subjects as varied as sports and dating. Among their adult books are two works of non-fiction and six novels.

Barbara and Scott have a remarkably happy marriage. They live in New York City with their stuffed polar bear, who is reputed to be a great wit.

About the Illustrator

Earl Norem has been a successful illustrator for many years. His work has appeared in Marvel Comics and Magazines, *Reader's Digest*, and many other publications. He and his family live in New Milford, Connecticut.

WIZARDS, WARRIORS, & YOU™

A new series of fantasy role-playing adventures
of skill, daring and danger that can be played over
and over again in each role—with a different
outcome every time!

In each WIZARDS, WARRIORS, & YOU™ adventure the
reader chooses the role of either the Wizard or the Warrior
before embarking on a perilous quest through a mythical
kingdom ruled by monsters and dragons.

As the Wizard, the reader takes the Book of Spells and is
master of all its mysterious, magical powers.

As the Warrior, the reader uses the Book of Weapons, a
complete arsenal of deadly arms, to prevail against all
challengers.